TURANDOT

Marianna Mayer • Winslow Pels

Morrow Junior Books
New York

Oil and oil pencil soluble were used for the full-color illustrations.
The text type is 16-point Cochin.

Library of Congress Cataloging-in-Publication Data
Mayer, Marianna.   Turandot/Marianna Mayer; illustrated by Winslow Pels.
p.   cm.   Based on the play by Carlo Gozzi.
Summary: Princess Turandot asks three riddles of her suitors, and only the one who answers
them correctly can become her husband.
ISBN 0-688-09073-7 (trade) — ISBN 0-688-09074-5 (library)
[1. Fairy tales.]   I. Pels, Winslow, ill.   II. Gozzi, Carlo, 1720–1806. Turandot.   III. Title.
PZ8.M4514Tu 1994   [E]—dc20   93-27033   CIP   AC

With love to Jennie Christensen and Lea,
for true friendship never dies
—M.M.

For Joshua and Jessica,
and Jill with the partridge eyes
—W.P.

In the city of Peking, China, there was a princess named Turandot who was famed for her beauty and many talents. She could sing like a nightingale, and her tales could charm even the dragon from its lair and the tiger from its prey.

Of course, such exceptional qualities brought Princess Turandot many suitors, though she cared for none. Indeed, if it were left to her, she would never marry.

Nevertheless, there came a time when her father, the emperor, insisted that she choose a husband. Turandot was quick to refuse, although it did her little good, for her father was as strong willed as she. Finally, the princess appeared to consent, but only under certain conditions, and these became the Law.

From that day forward, if a suitor wished to make Turandot his bride, he had to first strike the great bronze gong standing in the public square. Then, three riddles of Turandot's making would be posed to him. If he answered all three correctly, he would win her. If he failed, he must forfeit his life.

Turandot was convinced that the harsh Law would keep suitors away, yet it did not. To her great surprise, there were many young men willing to gamble their proud heads for a challenge. Their eagerness for the contest filled Turandot with contempt. She grew cold and her heart hardened against them, believing that they were desperate young men after not love or even her kingdom but the sheer thrill of risking all for some impossible goal.

In an effort to further discourage them, Turandot ordered that the head of each executed suitor be placed on view for everyone to see and be warned. Soon, along the high wall of the palace, there was evidence of the many suitors who had failed. No doubt this dismal display struck terror in the hearts of some, yet year after year still more suitors came.

Living in such an atmosphere, the people of Peking grew sullen and barbarous. They looked forward to each new suitor's failure and awaited each execution with grim enthusiasm.

As time passed, strange stories and beliefs concerning the princess sprang up among the people. They believed, for example, that the ghosts of her failed suitors haunted the city.

On nights of the full moon, if one dared listen, one might hear faint voices sing to Turandot:

"April did not blossom, nor did the snow melt. From the mountains to the vast oceans, do you not hear our voices, Princess? We who failed to prove our love, love you now and always will."

One evening, the sound of trumpets echoed within the public square, and a shiver of excitement struck the circle of people outside the palace gates, waiting to hear whether there would be a wedding or an execution.

Just then, the imperial mandarin appeared. "People of Peking," he called out. "The Persian prince has attempted to answer Princess Turandot's three riddles, but fortune was against him. Tonight, he shall die. *This is the Law.*"

As the mandarin finished speaking, the crowd surged forward, shouting, *"Sharpen the ax!"*

The imperial mandarin drew back, appalled. At that moment, the palace gates opened wide, and the imperial guard marched out to push back the crowd.

Caught up in the turmoil were two strangers to the city—Timur, the dethroned king of a distant land, and his son, Calaf. Fearing for his father, who was frail, Calaf quickly pulled him free from the wild crowd.

Once out of danger, Timur urged his son, "Let us leave this city. I fear no good will come of staying."

"But what is happening?" inquired Calaf.

"Never mind. Only let's—"

Suddenly, Timur was interrupted by the sounds of gongs, trumpets, and chimes. Silence fell in the public square.

At the same time, a cool wind swept through the city, and the fog began to lift. As the sky cleared, the full moon was revealed in all her luminous splendor. Moonlight streamed down, bathing the crowd in a cold silver glow. The eerie half-light caused Calaf to see everything as strangely dreamlike.

Presently, the palace gates opened again. Slowly,
mandarins, priests, and the executioner with his attendants
filed out into the dimly lit square. At last, the Persian prince

stepped out to follow. When the crowd saw him, they began to shout. But the prince looked neither right nor left. Instead, he seemed like a sleepwalker totally lost to those around him.

Abruptly, the crowd's enthusiasm for his execution dissolved, and they pitied him, saying, "Look how young he is."

"Why, he's little more than a boy!"

"Spare him!" they shouted. *"Mercy!"* they pleaded.

Timur took hold of Calaf's arm and insisted, "Here, my son. Come away now."

"Wait a little," replied Calaf, too intrigued to heed his father. When, finally, the Persian prince passed them, Calaf saw that the young prince's expression held no remorse or fear. His step was sure, his head was held high, and his dark eyes were aglow.

Continuing to call for mercy, the crowd hurried in pursuit of the procession. Try as he might, Timur could not prevent his son from joining the others.

"What sort of creature is this Princess Turandot that suitors gladly go to their death for her?" Calaf asked his father as they walked.

A man who had been following along behind them answered, "Some say it is the princess who should be pitied. But you must be strangers, for I have lived here all my life, and I have never seen either of you before."

"Yes, you are right," replied Calaf. "What do you know of these events?"

The man explained the rules of the competition, and then added, "It's a strange tale that some tell about her. You see, there are those among us who are filled with superstition. It is whispered that Turandot is under a spell. Some believe that on a whim the Moon Goddess froze the princess's heart. One day, they hope, the fire of love will thaw this ice princess. But I doubt that will ever happen."

By now the crowd had reached the executioner's block, and the people's shouts for mercy grew so loud that the princess stepped out onto the palace balcony to see what was happening.

Her cool, regal beauty stunned the shouting crowd, and they lowered their eyes and fell silent. Only three men remained gazing up at the princess—the Persian prince, Calaf, and the executioner.

Cold moonlight covered the princess's white-robed figure, causing her garments to shimmer. Slowly, she lifted one pale hand, then let it drop. That single imperious gesture sealed the fate of the Persian prince. The executioner bowed, knowing her meaning only too well. The Persian prince would receive no mercy.

Timur turned to his son and, seeing that a change had come over Calaf, reached out to him. "I pray that the sight of this cruel princess has not bewitched you." But Calaf was deaf to his words, so absorbed was he in the vision of Turandot.

"Speak to me," Timur demanded. "Tell me that I am mistaken."

"How can I," Calaf said at last, "when the sight of her fills my soul?"

"You are lost then!" groaned his father. "Just like the others."

"Father, you're wrong, for all at once to love her gives my life meaning."

"It will mean your death," said Timur.

Just then, in the distance, there was a call: *"Turandot!"* It was the voice of the Persian prince—his last word before dying.

"Would you die like him?" asked Timur.

"I will succeed, Father." With that, Calaf pulled free of Timur's hold and ran for the bronze gong, determined to summon the princess.

Suddenly, three figures sprang upon his path and barred his way. They were Ping, Pang, and Pong, the three ministers of Turandot.

"Go back!" they told him.

"If you wish to lose your head, go somewhere else to do it," said Pang.

"Our graveyards are full," said Ping.

"Let me pass!" demanded Calaf. But they would not.

"Go away," they said together.

Now at the same time, all around Calaf, phantom voices started to chant. "Don't delay," the phantoms whispered. "Strike the gong. Hurry! If you do, she will appear."

Looking up, Calaf saw these shadowy figures upon the palace ramparts. *"Hurry!"* they begged. "Don't delay!"

Calaf shuddered. He rubbed his eyes, wondering if these were ghosts. Might he be dreaming? It didn't matter. He made up his mind to strike the gong.

In one bold move, he broke away from the ministers and ran. Reaching the bronze gong, he took up the mallet and broke the silence, striking the gong three times.

The noise shook the public square and summoned

everyone, peasants and nobles, the royal court, and guards.
There were shouts and calls from the crowd. The Persian
prince was forgotten; all eyes were now on the new suitor.
Would he be the one to answer the riddles?

The doors to the palace opened, and the imperial guard came out to escort Calaf. Quickly, he was ushered into a magnificent hall, where the princess and her father awaited him.

The emperor spoke first. "Do you know the penalty should you answer any of the riddles incorrectly?"

"I do, Your Imperial Highness," replied Calaf, but his gaze was fixed on Turandot.

"Then let the riddles begin," ordered the emperor.

Refusing to meet his eyes, Turandot stepped forward and said, "The riddles are three; death is the result."

Calaf shook his head, saying, "The riddles are three; life is the result."

"We shall see," said Turandot. "This is the first riddle: In the dark night, a many-colored phantom flies. It soars and spreads its wings high above the gloomy crowd. People call to it, asking, begging favors. At dawn the phantom vanishes. Yet it is born again in each heart when darkness falls. And so it goes: Every night it soars anew, every day it dies. What is it?"

"It is *Hope,* for hope never vanishes for long. It will return," said Calaf.

Turandot stood frozen in silence, though for just an instant Calaf saw that his words caused her eyes to widen.

Ping, Pang, and Pong took up the scroll where she had written her answer. Solemnly, they unrolled the parchment and read aloud. "*Hope!* The answer is *Hope*," they shouted in unison. "He has answered the first riddle correctly."

"Yes," said Turandot in a voice as cold as the executioner's blade. "*Hope* is the answer. Hope that is merely illusion." In the next moment, she moved farther away from Calaf and sat down. "This is the second riddle—answer if you can. It burns like a flame, but it is not fire. Sometimes it smolders like a fever, but boredom will cool it. If you lose heart or die, it grows cold. Yet begin to dream, and the flame flares anew."

Calaf was silent. While he pondered, the three ministers whispered among themselves.

The minutes passed in silence, and the emperor, growing nervous, warned, "Your life hangs in the balance. Do answer if you can."

At last, Calaf said, "It is *Blood*! When you look at me, Princess, my blood seems to burn within me. Turn away, and the flame dies."

Turandot said nothing, but for a moment, reluctantly, her eyes held Calaf's gaze.

The three ministers unrolled the second scroll and read. "*Blood!*" they cried in concert. "Yes! He's right again!"

"Silence!" snapped Turandot as she got up to face Calaf. Slowly, she walked toward him, saying, "Here is the third and last riddle: What is the ice that gives you fire, and that your fire turns colder still? It is pearly white and black as night. If it welcomes you, you are its slave or *king*. Name this thing or die!"

At the nearness of her, Calaf dropped to his knees. "When you but turn your head and look at me, you cast a hundred spells."

"You're stalling with your flattery, stranger. You don't have the answer," Turandot concluded. "You're lost. Admit it. Ice that can create fire. What is it, or be done."

Jumping to his feet, Calaf said, "The answer is *Turandot*!"

The three ministers unrolled the last scroll. "Yes! He's right. He has won the challenge!" they shouted.

Turandot ran to her father's side. "Sweet Father, don't throw your only child into the arms of this stranger."

The emperor shook his head. "The Law is sacred, daughter."

"No! Don't say it. Spare me!" pleaded Turandot.

Again the emperor shook his head. "Your rules have been met. The Law is clear. By your own conditions, he has risked his life for you, and he has won."

"No! I will never agree," cried Turandot. Turning to Calaf, she asked, "Would you marry me even against my will?"

"No, only if you are willing," Calaf replied in a quiet voice. "But listen: You set three riddles before me. I'll put but one to you. What is my name? Give me the answer by tomorrow morning, and I'll leave this city with no further claim to you."

Stunned by the stranger's generosity, Turandot nodded and then swept from the hall. Wishing to be alone, Calaf went in search of a quiet place to pass the night. Once on the streets, he heard the heralds proclaiming, "By order of Princess Turandot, *tonight no one shall sleep in Peking. Whoever can give the name of the stranger who has won her challenge shall be rewarded. Whoever dares conceal it will receive death as punishment.*"

Seeking a spot beneath the stars where he might sleep awhile undisturbed, Calaf walked until he reached a forest beyond the city. There he came upon three shadowy figures huddled before an open fire.

Calaf made a move to turn away, but one of them called out, "So it's you." Calaf recognized the raspy voice at once; it was Ping's.

"We had to flee the palace," Pong informed him. "We've been besieged by that cold princess who snows upon our hearts with fearful threats and complaints."

"While you are out here contemplating the stars," Pang chimed in, "we've been tossing the bones of our ancestral dragons in the hope of discovering your name."

"Tell us your name, stranger," Ping begged. "Our lives are in your hands. There is no telling what she'll do if you refuse."

"Tell your princess she must find my name on her own or pay the price."

"She will not pay," all three assured him. "But we will give you anything you wish, if only you'll leave tonight," they suggested.

Calaf shook his head no.

"Look at what we can offer you," Pang said, and opened a chest filled with jewels and gold. "It's a fortune! How can you refuse?"

"No," said Calaf. "I shall have Turandot or nothing. She is all I want."

"You won't have her," they insisted, and with that, the three ministers turned away, leaving Calaf alone.

After walking some distance toward the palace in silence, Ping said, "For the first time in my life, something has changed within me."

Pang concurred. "That young man surprises me."

"I look on love without sneering," Pong concluded, "because of his conviction."

"I cannot remember feeling this way," confided Ping. "Why, I wish him to succeed!"

"Yes," agreed Pang. "If only she could love him. But that is impossible."

The next morning, at dawn, Calaf returned to the palace. "Princess of Ice," he called. "Come down from your pedestal. It's time to give me your answer."

In the great hall, they stood alone together. While they silently gazed at each other, Turandot felt her resolve to hate Calaf weaken. Yet she feared him because he had won her grudging respect. "It appears you are both brave and generous," she said. "Tell me, what can I do to be free of you?"

"You need only ask, Princess. I cannot refuse you."

"Then what is your secret? You know mine. From the moment I saw you, I knew you were not like the others." Turandot turned away from him, and tears filled her eyes. "My first tears," she whispered to herself.

Turning back to Calaf, she said, "I despised the others, but I fear you. I'm torn and divided; conquer you or be conquered. Is this not victory enough?"

"No, for I have no wish to hurt you," said Calaf in a voice filled with sadness.

"Then leave me my dignity and give me my freedom," Turandot begged.

"Very well. I will make you a gift, though you may doom us both if you choose to use it. My name is Prince Calaf, son of King Timur, yet I am without lands and throne."

All at once the trumpets sounded, and the emperor and court officials, ministers and peasants alike filled the great hall, anxious to witness the final contest.

"The time has come," said the emperor. "Do you know the stranger's name?"

"Yes, Father," Turandot began, "I do." And turning to look into Calaf's eyes, she said, "His name is...*Love*."

Calaf ran to Turandot and embraced her. "Together we'll bring an end to fear, and Love will be the only law of the land," she promised him.

There were cheers from the crowd and sighs of relief from the ministers.

"Love has made the tiger and the dragon come to rest side by side in harmony," said the emperor.

A wedding celebration was ordered by the emperor, and Ping, Pang, and Pong hurried to arrange the ceremony.

Soon, all of Peking looked like a magic forest with flowering trees and exotic shrubs. On top of the palace, temple roofs, and gate houses, vivid scarlet banners danced in the breeze. At dusk, crimson lanterns lit the handsome painted pavilions and ornate arches, and rose petals were showered over the streets of the city.

On the day of the wedding, Turandot joined her hand
with Calaf's, and together they made their vows, promising
to love and keep each other as they would cherish the land
they ruled.

In the years that followed, the land held the weight of their love as a tree blossoms and bears fruit. Surrounded by such newfound love, the people flourished, knowing peace as never before.

Author's Note

The best-known and probably the oldest story of the proud princess who tests her suitors with riddles is that of Turandot, a tale of Persian origin included in the *Thousand and One Nights*. As *Turandotte*, the story was dramatized for the theater in 1762 by the celebrated Italian playwright Carlo Gozzi. Subsequently, *Turandotte* was adapted as an opera by a number of composers, including Antonio Bazzini, Ferruccio Busoni, Adolph Jensen, and Karl Reissiger.

However, it is Giacomo Puccini's opera composition that has made *Turandot* most famous. This opera was considered his most dramatic and complex work. Begun in 1920, Puccini's score was left unfinished at his death, in 1924. The task of completion went to composer Franco Alfano, who added a duet and the concluding scene, and it is this version that is performed today. The character of the faithful slave girl, Liù, is Puccini's invention and cannot be found in any of the other versions.

In the area of folklore, the Brothers Grimm included a *Turandot* variant, entitled *The Sea-hare (Das Meerhäschen)*, in a final (1857) edition, having taken it from a collection of German folktales from Transylvania published the previous year by Joseph Haltrich in Berlin.

JAN 1 0 2003